I'm too small.

YOU'RE TOO BIG.

by JUDI BARRETT
illustrated by
David Rose

ATHENEUM 1981 NEW YORK

LIBRARY OF CONGRESS CATALOGING IN PUBLICATION DATA

Barrett, Judith.
I'm too small, you're too big.

SUMMARY: Text and pictures contrast the size
differences between Daddy and son and point out that
though being small is frustrating, it has
some advantages.
[1. Size and shape—Fiction]   I. Rose,
David S., 1947-   II. Title.
PZ7.B2752Im   [E]   80-23883
ISBN 0-689-30800-0

Story copyright © 1981 by Judith Barrett
Illustrations copyright © 1981 by David S. Rose
All rights reserved
Published simultaneously in Canada by
McClelland & Stewart, Ltd.
Printed by Connecticut Printers, Hartford, Connecticut
Bound by A. Horowitz & Sons, Fairfield, New Jersey
Designed by mutual consent
First Edition

Dedicated to all sizes.

I'm too small
to be a grown-up.
BUT YOU'RE TOO BIG
TO BE A KID.

I'm too small
to wear your shoes.

BUT YOU'RE TOO BIG
TO WEAR MY DRACULA COSTUME.

I'm to small
to go to the moon.

BUT YOU'RE TOO BIG
TO GO TO DAY CAMP.

I'm too small
to drive your car.

BUT YOU'RE TOO BIG
TO DRIVE MY TRICYCLE.

I'm too small
to reach the top of the table.

BUT YOU'RE TOO BIG
TO HIDE OUT UNDERNEATH IT.

I'm too small
to stay in the house all by myself.

BUT YOU'RE TOO BIG
TO HAVE A BABYSITTER.

I'm too small
to see over the top of the fence.

BUT YOU'RE TOO BIG
TO SIT ON TOP OF MY SHOULDERS.

I'm too small
to climb a mountain.

BUT YOU'RE TOO BIG
TO CLIMB MY JUNGLEGYM.

I'm too small
to play in the Big Leagues.

BUT YOU'RE TOO BIG
TO PLAY IN THE LITTLE LEAGUES.

I'm too small
to go to work.

BUT YOU'RE TOO BIG
TO GO TO KINDERGARTEN.

I'm too small
to swim in deep water.

BUT YOU'RE TOO BIG
TO FIT INTO MY RUBBER DRAGON.

I'm too small
to build a house.

BUT YOU'RE TOO BIG
TO PLAY HOUSE.

I'm too small
to go to your parties.

BUT YOU'RE TOO BIG
TO GO TO MY PARTIES.

But someday I'll be as big as you are.

MAYBE EVEN BIGGER.